Yogurt the Ogre

The Big Tale of the Not-So-Tidy Whale

Driven by optimism, fun, playfulness, and exploration, pdoink seeks to inspire families
to transform, perform, and grow. pdoink invents and realizes great stories that
enable learning and enjoyment for positive change and self-development.

The positively pdoinkian adventures of Yogurt the Ogre are timeless tales of self-reflection and
friendship led by a re-imagined ogre. We created these stories to help children learn
to care about people, the world around them, and themselves!

Because we are parents, we understand bedtime. The Big Tale of the Not-So-Tidy Whale is a terrific 7 o'clock
story to share with your children. Read on, and you'll also find one of Yogurt's favorite tales at the end
of each book. While children love to read stories about Yogurt and his friends, Yogurt's favorite
poems are about children. These fun poems are designed to enhance the reading experience
for your children and, in a pinch, they make a great 8 o'clock story. Enjoy!

———————————

Yogurt the Ogre created by David Rendimonti
Bedtime Stories for Yogurt the Ogre created by Lawrence Hourihan
Yogurt the Ogre–The Big Tale of the Not-So-Tidy Whale published by Shawna Sheldon
Writing by David Rendimonti, Lawrence Hourihan, Jessica Lowe, and Shawna Sheldon
Illustration by Agnes Garbowska
Book design by Gillian and Paul Sych

For our families—DR and LH

Please visit us at: www.pdoink.com

pdo!nk

Published by pdo!nk Inc., Toronto, Ontario, Canada.

ISBN 978-0-9868013-0-3

This book was printed in Toronto, Canada, by C.J. Graphics Inc., www.cjgraphics.com,
using solar energy, wind power, and bio-derived inks, and on paper that has been certified
by the Forest Stewardship Council and supported by the Rainforest Alliance.

10 9 8 7 6 5 4 3 2 1

yogurt the ogre

The Big Tale of the Not-So-Tidy Whale

A very wise stone, Mr. Granite Mosstop, lay near a brook in Mudd Hollow, watching and thinking about the world and the way it should be. Such is the way of all things that are rock-solid.

On this wet day, he gazed at the shiny dew and watched as Sunshine continued her busy work of changing the wet forest into a bright and sparkly playground.

Over his many years, Granite Mosstop had seen all that was happy and all that was sad, all that was good and all that was bad. Mosstop was a happy and comfortable rock, but he rarely smiled.

He was old and quiet and wise, but mostly he was tired.

Mosstop was startled by the sound of some very loud and delightful laughter.

"Who is that disturbing my peace and quiet?" he asked.

Down the winding path of Mudd Hollow bounced a young and tiny ogre, skipping and splashing in the puddles and waving his arms in the air.

Whoosh!

"I am the biggest whale in the world and my tail can make waves that reach up to the sky!"

Spliish! splash! spluck!

A glop of mud landed on Mosstop's face.

"Hey! What are you doing, young one? Please show some care for those around you," said Mosstop.

"Oh! Uh, who are you?" fumbled Yogurt.

"I might ask the same of you," stated old Mosstop.

"I am Yogurt!" said Yogurt with great pride. "But today I am a giant blue whale!"

Yogurt the Ogre, thought the stone, *now that is a funny name*, and he cracked a little smile.

"Ouch"!

"What happened, Mr. Rock?"

"My name, young ogre, is Granite Mosstop... and I believe I may have hurt myself smiling. You see, I have not smiled in some time."

That's weird, thought Yogurt. "Well, Mr. Mosstop, I always feel good when I smile."

"Oops," said Yogurt.

"Hey!" said Mosstop.

Then, just as swiftly as he had arrived, Yogurt was off. "Gotta go," he declared and away he bounced. "Nice meeting you Mr. Mosstop."

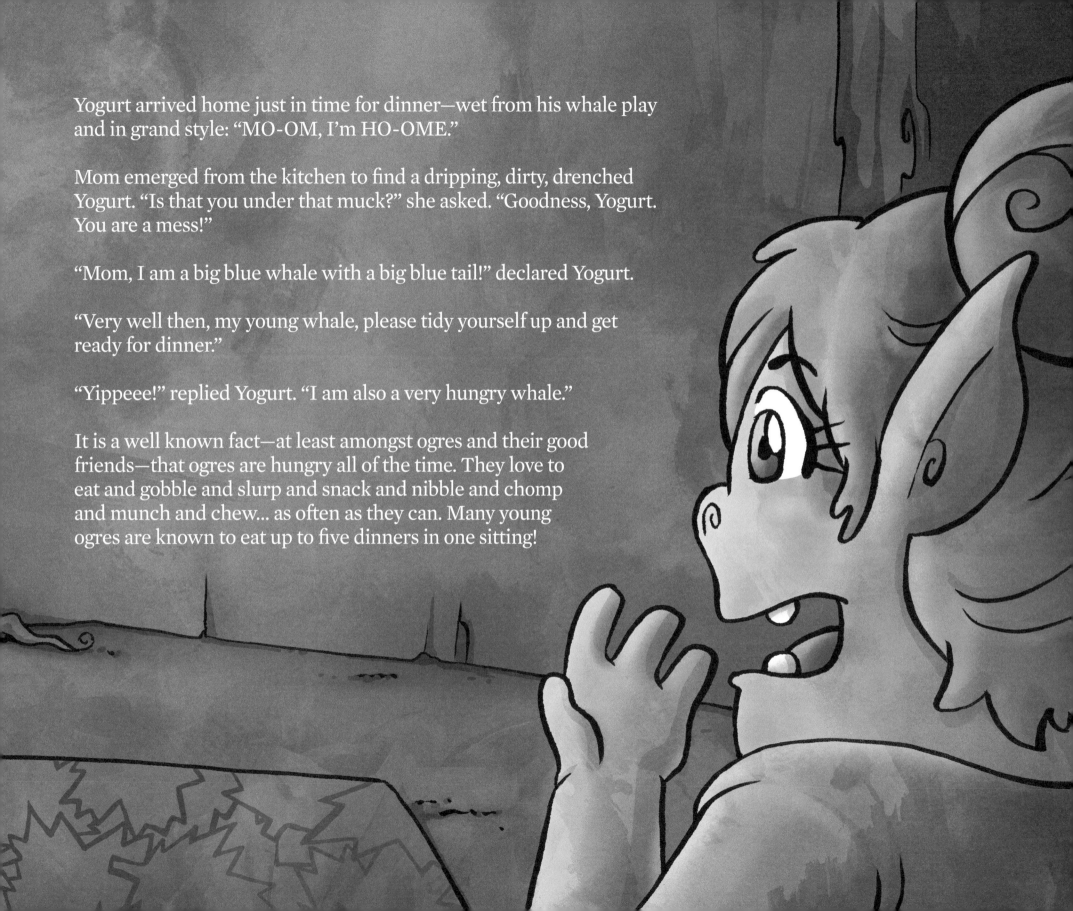

Yogurt arrived home just in time for dinner—wet from his whale play and in grand style: "MO-OM, I'm HO-OME."

Mom emerged from the kitchen to find a dripping, dirty, drenched Yogurt. "Is that you under that muck?" she asked. "Goodness, Yogurt. You are a mess!"

"Mom, I am a big blue whale with a big blue tail!" declared Yogurt.

"Very well then, my young whale, please tidy yourself up and get ready for dinner."

"Yippeee!" replied Yogurt. "I am also a very hungry whale."

It is a well known fact—at least amongst ogres and their good friends—that ogres are hungry all of the time. They love to eat and gobble and slurp and snack and nibble and chomp and munch and chew... as often as they can. Many young ogres are known to eat up to five dinners in one sitting!

Pdoink!

Yogurt's spoon plopped into his bowl of soup.

Up into the air went a splash of soup.

splat!

Down onto the table plopped a mess of soup.

"Please be a good ogre and eat your soup," said Dad.
"There will be plenty of time for playing later."

"Okay Dad, you know... it's just that I'm a hungry
whale and whales like to splash."

"Yes, Yogurt. I know. But right now you are
Yogurt the Ogre and you need to be more
careful. Please be tidy at the table."

Splish!

"Oops!" cried Yogurt.

"Yogurt Yorrick Yeardly Ogre!"

Yogurt knew that when Mom and Dad used
all of his names, it was not a good thing...

...and Yogurt was right.

"Yogurt, you really need to try harder to be tidy.
Look at the mess you're making," said Yogurt's mom.

"If you're finished with your dinner, dear, then it's
time for your bath."

All young ogres loved bath time, especially Yogurt, and
off he scampered to the bathtub for more water fun.

"Do be careful, Yogurt!" his mom shouted as Yogurt
bounced down the hall.

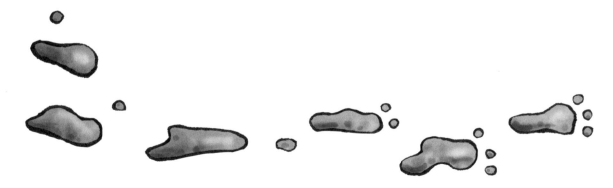

sploosh!

This time the great blue whale dove deep
under the water holding his breath and
looking for other fish to play with.

Whoosh! Out popped Yogurt with a big wave of his arms.

Splat! Down came a plop of soapy water...

...onto the bathroom floor.

"Oh dear!" said Yogurt's mom. "There is water ALL over the bathroom!"

"Yogurt, please-hop-out-of-the-bath-at-once-and-dry-off-and-brush-your-hair-and-brush-your-teeth-and-put-on-your-pyjamas-for-bed," added Dad.

Yogurt knew that when Mom and Dad made a whole bunch of words into one word, it was not a good thing...

...and Yogurt was right.

Young Yogurt had only wanted to play. He had never meant to upset his mom and dad. After all, it was just good fun. Besides, how could he have known the big blue whale could cause such a mess?

"You know, Yogurt," said his mom when she was tucking him into bed, "It's good to have fun, but it's easy to get carried away. You should always pay attention to those around you. What might seem like fun for you may not be so fun for others... and it is not fun for those of us who are left cleaning up the mess that you leave behind."

Yogurt pulled a bedtime story from his shelf, hopped into bed, and thought for a long, long, long, long time about what his mom had said.

Soon he began drifting off, and Moonbeam's soft glow helped soothe a troubled Yogurt to sleep.

The next morning, Yogurt awoke to the bright, warm sunshine, and he set off for a stroll through the forest. As he walked, he thought about what had happened the night before. He knew that Mom and Dad were disappointed with him, but he didn't really understand why.

Along the journey, Yogurt happened upon his new friend, Granite Mosstop. Granite was quietly resting in the morning sun.

The previous day's rain had left large greenish, brownish puddles on the forest floor, and Yogurt very carefully tiptoed in and out of the puddles and past Mr. Mosstop.

Suddenly...

Whoosh!

Out of the bushes, at top speed, bolted Tumbleberry Bunny, Copper Caterpillar, and Lady Blue Damselfly.

It was a well known fact that Tumbleberry Bunny was the most carefree and reckless of merry-makers in Mudd Hollow. She and her friends were deep into a game of touch tag, and Lady Blue was 'it.'

"Catch me if you can!" laughed Tumbleberry, and she disappeared into the forest with Lady Blue close behind.

Splish, Splash, Splat!

Yogurt tried to take cover, but he was not able to jump out of the way in time. He was speckled with mud from head to toe. He spit out a mouthful of muck and turned to see a splattered Mosstop. His friend had been startled awake... and he was not happy.

Yogurt looked down at his mud-covered body and then at Mosstop. As he approached Mosstop, he was reminded of the chat that he'd had the night before with his mom. *Indeed*, he thought, *what seems like fun for some is not always fun for others.*

He helped Mosstop wipe the mud from his face.

"Mr. Mosstop, I'm sorry I splashed you yesterday," said Yogurt.

And then he paused… *And I believe I owe Mom and Dad an apology for the messes I left behind yesterday*, he thought.

"Well Yogurt, yes, you did splash me yesterday. I know that sometimes we get carried away when we are playing. It's hard to be a *tidy*, giant blue whale, but it is important to try."

Yogurt leaned over, wrapped his arms around his new friend, and gave him the biggest, warmest hug—the only kind of hug he knew how to give.

"Thank you, Mr. Mosstop," he said, and he dashed down the path and headed for home.

As Yogurt disappeared into the forest, Mosstop smiled—with a little less pain—and very quietly whispered, "And thank *you*, little ogre for reminding me how much fun it is to have fun."

That night, Mom and Dad gave Yogurt an extra special hug when they tucked him into bed with his bedtime story. When the lights went out, he thought for a moment about the wonderful day he'd had. Moonbeam smiled down on Yogurt in his warm cozy bed, and Yogurt soon drifted to sleep to dream wonderful dreams of tidy whales with not-so-giant tails.

PERRY'S PLAYGROUND

A Bedtime Story for Yogurt the Ogre

At Sunnyday School
The bell chimed 'RING, RING'!
All dashed to the playground
To slide and to swing.

A young boy named Perry,
Much taller than the rest,
Was gentle but clumsy,
Some called him a pest.

Perry had three good friends:
Mary, Terry, and Carrie.
They all were quite nice,
Yet some found them scary.

The foursome began
A quick game of flag tag.
Each stuffing their pockets
With bright colored rags.

"Ready or not!"
Perry called happily.
And he ran towards Mary,
As fast as could be!

She slid down the slide
As he dove through the air.
He reached for her flag,
But he missed by a hair!

A small boy slid next,
Perry right on his tail.
They crashed with a SMACK!
The boy let out a wail.

Up high in the air,
He rose like a balloon.
Then tumbling down,
With a CRASH and a BOOM!

But Perry just ran,
He did not even pause.
He moved like the wind,
And ran past the seesaws.

He dashed towards Terry,
Whose flag flashed bright blue.
They pushed past the swings,
But they barely squeezed through!

A child on the swing
Spun round like a top!
Whirling and twirling
'Til she came to a stop!

Then Perry changed course
And sprinted to Carrie,
Who swung from the monkey bars
Then flew like a fairy.

But as Perry followed
His legs kicked and thrashed.
Five children were knocked,
They all dangled and crashed!

At last Perry made it
But as he jumped down,
He heard a loud 'TWEET'
And saw his teacher's frown.

"Look around Perry,
No children will play!
Your game's fun for you,
But scared others away!

Please be more careful.
The playground's for all!
Each boy and each girl,
Tall, short, big, and small!"

Perry thought for a while
On what had been said.
Walked back to his friends
They huddled head to head.

After a moment
And to the teacher's surprise,
The four walked to the others
And spoke words so wise:

"We're SORRY!" they cried.
"If we hurt or scared you.
If you'd like to join us,
Then you can play too!"

So every child chose
Their own bright colored rag.
And together they played,
A game of flag tag!